Rainbow Fish & Friends

THE COPYCAT FISH

TEXT BY GAIL DONOVAN
ILLUSTRATIONS BY DAVID AUSTIN CLAR STUDIO

Night Sky Books
New York • London

The new school year was about to begin and Rainbow Fish
and his friends were swimming around in excited circles.

"Attention, please!" called Miss Cuttle. "When I call your name, please swim into the cave so we can start. Rainbow Fish?"

"Here!" answered Rainbow Fish, flipping his special loop-the-loop past the teacher.

As Miss Cuttle called the roll, Dyna, Puffer, Rusty, Spike, Rosie, Pearl, and Little Blue crowded into the school cave. "Tug?"

Mustering up his courage, Tug tried flipping into the cave just like Rainbow Fish. "I'm here!" he said, tumbling into Miss Cuttle.

"I can see that." She smiled.

Hey, that's my special move! thought Rainbow Fish.

First thing that morning, Miss Cuttle asked the younger students to sort shells by size, from tiny baby ones to giant surf clams. The older students counted out pebbles into sets of ten.

Rainbow Fish had an idea. He counted out ten pebbles and arranged them in a triangle. Then he counted out ten more in the shape of a square. Making shapes was more fun than making plain old piles, and he was still doing his task.

Tug looked over to see what the big fish were doing. Rainbow Fish's shapes looked like more fun than his own straight line. He started pushing the line of shells into a big circle.

"Stop!" cried Little Blue. "That's not how you're supposed to do it!"

Miss Cuttle hurried over. "Tug, I was hoping we could create a line of shells to measure. Next time, let's pay attention to our own tasks."

At snack time, Miss Cuttle offered algae or krill. Rainbow Fish chose algae and quickly swam off so that Tug couldn't see what he had picked.

"I want whatever Rainbow Fish has," Tug admitted.

"Looks like we've got ourselves a copycat fish!" Spike laughed.

Rainbow Fish scurried back. "I've changed my mind," he said. "I want krill."

"Me, too," said Tug quickly. "I want krill, too."

Miss Cuttle put all the algae away. "Everyone will have krill today," she said. "And next time, I want each fish to choose for him or herself."

"Attention!" called Miss Cuttle. "This afternoon, we'll be creating a garden. I've divided you up into teams. Rosie, Spike, and Puffer, you'll do the digging. Little Blue and Dyna, you'll take care of raking. Pearl and Rusty, you'll be in charge of the garden's border. Tug and Rainbow Fish, you'll team up to do the planting."

Rainbow Fish couldn't believe his bad luck. Miss Cuttle had put him with the copycat!

Tug pestered Rainbow Fish with questions. "What should we plant first? Where should we plant it?"

There was nowhere for Rainbow Fish to hide his work. Nowhere for Rainbow Fish to hide himself. He felt trapped. Trying to ignore Tug, he shoved plants any which way in the holes. He wished he could shove Tug into a hole.

Tug swam alongside Rainbow Fish. "What should I do?"

"Do what you want!" shouted Rainbow Fish. "You do it your way and I'll do it mine!"

Tug swam away sadly, then turned around and came back. "But your way always looks like so much more fun than anyone else's, that's the only reason I copy."

"Well you wouldn't like it if someone always copied you!" cried Rainbow Fish.

"I don't know," said Tug. "I think it's fun to do things together. When I'm older and the little ones copy me, I think I'll like it!"

Rainbow Fish felt mixed up. Part of him still felt boiling mad at Tug, but another part could see what Tug meant. He didn't know what to do. He looked across the garden and suddenly realized what he had created—a big mess! "I've ruined it!" he cried.

"Wait a minute," said Tug. "I have an idea. What if we put the tall ones in the back and the short ones in the front, just like when we sorted clamshells?"

"That's a great idea!" said Rainbow Fish.

"I'm very proud of each and every one of you for working together to create such a beautiful garden," said Miss Cuttle at the end of the day.

Rainbow Fish felt so happy as he floated through their beautiful new garden that he looped-the-loop for a good-bye flip.

Then the others followed, admiring their work.

Last came Tug. Remembering that Rainbow Fish had liked his idea made Tug so happy that he zoomed ahead to say good-bye to him. He had to zig and zag around the other fish. It was so much fun he did it again—zoom and zig and zag.

"Hey, nice move!" yelled Spike.

"Want to swim home together?" asked Rainbow Fish. "I can show you how to do my flip and maybe you can show me how to do that zigzag."

"Sure," said Tug, and he and Rainbow Fish swam side by side all the way home.